An Anta Adventure

by Ann Shepard

Strategy Focus

As you read, **monitor** how well you understand what is happening. Reread to **clarify** parts that seem unclear.

 HOUGHTON MIFFLIN   BOSTON

Key Vocabulary

barren almost no plant or animal life

crevasse a deep hole or crack

deserted having few or no people living in it

floes large pieces of floating ice

grueling tiring and very hard to do

impassable not able to be crossed or traveled through

perilous very dangerous

terrain land, ground, or earth

Word Teaser

What vocabulary word rhymes with two parts of your body?

The New Explorers

Antarctica is a continent at the bottom of the world. Most of Antarctica is covered in ice. Only a few scientists live there.

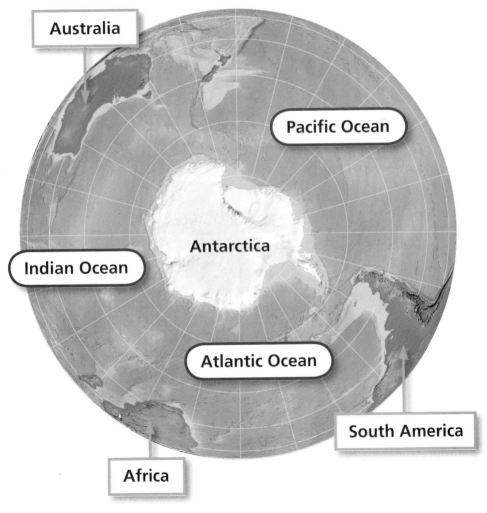

Australia

Pacific Ocean

Indian Ocean

Antarctica

Atlantic Ocean

South America

Africa

Ann Bancroft and Liv Arnesen both wanted to visit Antarctica.

Both women love to explore in perilous, or dangerous, places!

Planning the Trip

Ann and Liv had never met. They knew that a trip across Antarctica would be grueling, or very hard.

Each woman wanted to go with a partner. So Ann asked Liv if she was interested in the trip. Of course Liv said yes!

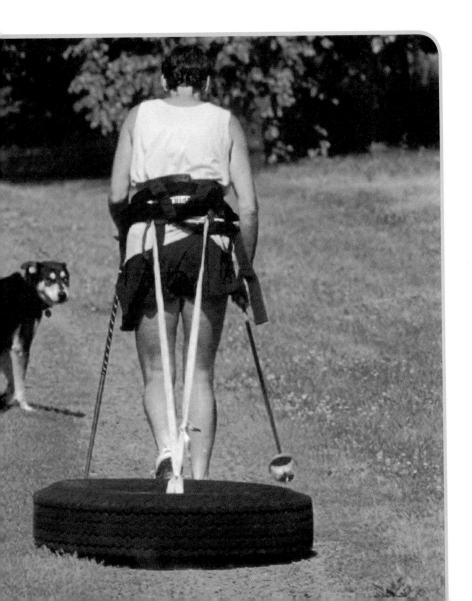

The Start

On November 13, 2000, a plane dropped Ann Bancroft and Liv Arnesen off at the edge of Antarctica. They were now in a barren, icy land. No plants grew there.

Antarctica is deserted except for scientists, penguins and other birds, and animals.

The women crossed many kinds of terrain. Their path took them up and down mountains. They crossed wide areas of ice and snow.

The most dangerous part of the trip was a river of ice called a glacier. Anyone who falls into a crevasse, or deep crack, might be killed. Some crevasses were impassable. They just could not be crossed.

crevasse

The End of the Adventure

On February 11, 2001, Ann and Liv pulled their sleds onto the Ross Ice Shelf. They had traveled 1,700 miles! A ship was waiting another 500 miles away to take Ann and Liv home.

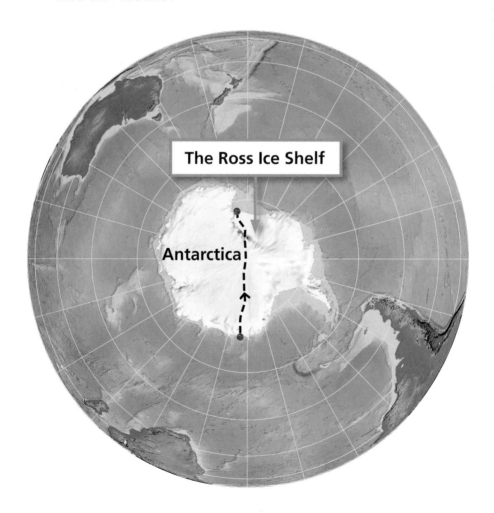

The Ross Ice Shelf

Antarctica

But winter was setting in. Ice floes were forming in the water. Soon these floating pieces of ice would freeze together and trap the ship. The ship had to leave without them.

Making History

A plane carried Ann and Liv home from their great adventure. Ann Bancroft and Liv Arnesen became the first women to cross Antarctica. Together, they made history!

NOTE

Responding

Putting Words to Work

1. If you visited a **barren, deserted** place, what would you expect to see there?

2. Choose two of the photos in this book. How do the photos help you understand how **perilous** the **terrain** of Antarctica is?

3. What would you do if you came to an **impassable** place in a road?

4. Describe something **grueling** that you or someone else has done.

5. **PARTNER ACTIVITY:** Think of a word you learned in the text. Explain its meaning to your partner and give an example.

Answer to Word Teaser
Floes rhymes with *nose* and *toes*.